Bad Rat!

Level 1A

Written by Karen Wallace
Illustrated by Rachael O'Neill

Ticktock

What is synthetic phonics?

Synthetic phonics teaches children to recognise the sounds of letters and to blend 'synthesise' them together to make whole words.

Understanding sound/letter relationships gives children the confidence and ability to read unfamiliar words, without having to rely on memory or guesswork; this helps them progress towards independent reading.

Did you know? Spoken English uses more than 40 speech sounds. Each sound is called a *phoneme*. Some phonemes relate to a single letter (d-o-g) and others to combinations of letters (sh-ar-p). When a phoneme is written down it is called a *grapheme*. Teaching these sounds, matching them to their written form and sounding out words for reading is the basis of synthetic phonics.

Consultant

I love reading phonics has been created in consultation
with language expert Abigail Steel. She has a
background in teaching and teacher training and is
a respected expert in the field of Synthetic Phonics.
Abigail Steel is a regular contributor to educational
publications. Her international education consultancy
supports parents and teachers in the promotion of
literacy skills.

Reading tips

This book focuses on the sounds:
s, a, t, p, i, n, c, e, h, r, m, d, g, o, u, l, f and b.

Tricky words in this book

Any words in bold may have unusual spellings or are new and have not yet been introduced.

> ### Tricky words in this book:
>
> **my   said   to   the**
> **I   see   you   me**

Extra ways to have fun with this book

After the reader has finished the story, ask them questions about what they have just read:

Where did Rat hide?
Why was Rat's behaviour bad?

Make flashcards of the focus sounds (s, a, t, p, i, n, c, e, h, r, m, d, g, o, u, l, f and b). Ask the reader to say the sounds. This will help reinforce letter/sound matches.

Reading is fun!
I love to read with my mum, snuggled up in bed. She always says *"Well done!"* when I read.

A pronunciation guide

 This grid highlights the sounds used in the story and offers a guide on how to say them.

s as in sat	a as in ant	t as in tin
p as in pig	i as in ink	n as in net
c as in cat	e as in egg	h as in hen
r as in rat	m as in mug	d as in dog
g as in get	o as in ox	u as in up
l as in log	f as in fan	b as in bag

Be careful not to add an 'uh' sound to 's', 't', 'p', 'c', 'h', 'r', 'm', 'd', 'g', 'l', 'f' and 'b'. For example, say 'fff' not 'fuh' and 'sss' not 'suh'.

Rat hid a bun in his bed.

'**My** bun!' **said** Pig **to** Fat Cat.

'**The** bad rat has my bun!'

'Let **me** get Rat!' said Fat Cat.

Fat Cat ran to the red hut.

Rat hid in a pot!

Rat hid in a hat!

Rat hid in a mug!

Fat Cat sat on the rug.

'I can **see you**, Rat,' said Fat Cat.
Tug! Tug!

'Get me the bun, Rat. Pig is mad,'
said Fat Cat.

'The bun is in the bed,' said Rat.

Pig has his bun.

Bad Rat!

OVER **48** TITLES IN SIX LEVELS
Abigail Steel recommends...

Other titles to enjoy from Level 1

I love reading phonics — Clint and Grant Play I-Spy
978-1-78325-098-1

I love reading phonics — The Best Gift
978-1-84898-603 9

I love reading phonics — Gran and Bret's Trip
978-1-78325-100-1

Some titles from Level 2

I love reading phonics — Wish Fish
978-1-84898-604-6

I love reading phonics — Chuck and Duck
978-1-84898-605-3

I love reading phonics — Pink Bunny
978-1-78325-103-2

I love reading phonics — Let's go to the Swings
978-1-78325-102-5

Some titles from Level 3

I love reading phonics — Bart's Go-Cart
978-1-78325-105-6

I love reading phonics — Queen Ella's Feet
978-1-84898-609-1

I love reading phonics — Puff Flies
978-1-84898-610-7

I love reading phonics — The Pop Duel
978-1-78325-108-7

An Hachette UK Company
www.hachette.co.uk

Copyright © Octopus Publishing Group Ltd 2012
First published in Great Britain in 2012 by TickTock, an imprint of Octopus Publishing Group Ltd,
Endeavour House, 189 Shaftesbury Avenue, London WC2H 8JY.
www.octopusbooks.co.uk
www.ticktockbooks.co.uk

ISBN 978 1 84898 600 8

Printed and bound in China
10 9 8 7 6 5 4 3

All rights reserved. No part of this work may be reproduced or utilised in any form or by any means, electronic or mechanical, including photocopying, recording or by any information storage and retrieval system, without the prior written permission of the publisher.